THE ELEPHANT'S CHILD

RUDYARD KIPLING

THE

ILLUSTRATIONS BY LORINDA BRYAN CAULEY

ELEPHANT'S CHILD

HARCOURT BRACE JOVANOVICH, PUBLISHERS   SAN DIEGO • NEW YORK • LONDON

Other picture books
illustrated by Lorinda Bryan Cauley

THE UGLY DUCKLING
by Hans Christian Andersen

THE GOOSE AND THE GOLDEN COINS
by Giambattista Basile

OLD HIPPO'S EASTER EGG
by Jan Wahl

THE GOODNIGHT CIRCLE
by Carolyn Lesser

THE BEGINNING OF THE ARMADILLOS
by Rudyard Kipling

PUSS IN BOOTS
by Charles Perrault

Copyright © 1983 by Lorinda Bryan Cauley
Designed by Barbara DuPree Knowles

Requests for permission to make copies of any part of the work should be mailed to: Permissions, Harcourt Brace Jovanovich, Publishers, Orlando, Florida 32887.

Library of Congress Cataloging in Publication Data

Kipling, Rudyard, 1865-1936. The elephant's child.
Summary: Because of his " 'satiable curtiosity" about what the crocodile has for dinner, the elephant's child and all elephants thereafter have long trunks.
[1. Elephants—Fiction] I. Cauley, Lorinda Bryan, ill.   II. Title.
PZ7.K632E1   1983   [E]   82-21266

ISBN 0-15-332878-9   (Library: 10 different titles)
ISBN 0-15-332922-X   (Single title, 4 copies)
ISBN 0-15-332982-3   (Replacement single copy)

For my brother Karl with love   —L. B. C.

In the High and Far-Off Times the Elephant, O Best Beloved, had no trunk. He had only a blackish, bulgy nose, as big as a boot, that he could wriggle about from side to side; but he couldn't pick up things with it. But there was one Elephant—a new Elephant— an Elephant's Child—who was full of 'satiable curtiosity, and that means he asked ever so many questions. *And* he lived in Africa, and he filled all Africa with his 'satiable curtiosities.

He asked his tall aunt, the Ostrich, why her tail-feathers grew just so, and his tall aunt, the Ostrich, spanked him with her hard, hard claw.

He asked his tall uncle,
the Giraffe, what made
his skin spotty, and his
tall uncle, the Giraffe,
spanked him with
his hard, hard hoof.
And still he was full
of 'satiable curtiosity!

He asked his broad aunt, the Hippopotamus, why her eyes were red, and his broad aunt, the Hippopotamus, spanked him with her broad, broad hoof;

and he asked his hairy uncle, the Baboon, why melons tasted just so, and his hairy uncle, the Baboon, spanked him with his hairy, hairy paw. And *still* he was full of 'satiable curtiosity! He asked questions about everything that he saw, or heard, or felt, or smelt, or touched, and all his uncles and his aunts spanked him. And still he was full of 'satiable curtiosity!

One fine morning in the middle of the Precession of the Equinoxes this 'satiable Elephant's Child asked a new fine question that he had never asked before. He asked, "What does the Crocodile have for dinner?" Then everybody said, "Hush!" in a loud and dretful tone, and they spanked him immediately and directly, without stopping, for a long time.

By and by, when that was finished, he came upon Kolokolo Bird sitting in the middle of a wait-a-bit thorn-bush, and he said, "My father has spanked me, and my mother has spanked me; all my aunts and uncles have spanked me for my 'satiable curtiosity; and *still* I want to know what the Crocodile has for dinner!"

Then Kolokolo Bird said, with a mournful cry, "Go to the banks of the great grey-green, greasy Limpopo River, all set about with fever-trees, and find out."

That very next morning, when there was nothing left of the Equinoxes, because the Precession had preceded according to precedent, this 'satiable Elephant's Child took a hundred pounds of bananas (the little short red kind), and a hundred pounds of sugar-cane (the long purple kind), and seventeen melons (the greeny-crackly kind), and said to all his dear families, "Good-bye. I am going to the great grey-green, greasy Limpopo River, all set about with fever-trees, to find out what the Crocodile has for dinner." And they all spanked him once more for luck, though he asked them most politely to stop.

Then he went away, a little warm, but not at all astonished, eating melons and throwing the rind about, because he could not pick it up.

He went from Graham's Town to Kimberley, and from Kimberley to Khama's Country, and from Khama's Country he went east by north, eating melons all the time, till at last he came to the banks of the great grey-green, greasy Limpopo River, all set about with fever-trees, precisely as Kolokolo Bird had said.

Now you must know and understand, O Best Beloved, that till that very week, and day, and hour, and minute, this 'satiable Elephant's Child had never seen a Crocodile and did not know what one was like. It was all his 'satiable curtiosity.

The first thing that he found was a Bi-Coloured-
Python-Rock-Snake curled round a rock.

" 'Scuse me," said the Elephant's Child most politely, "but have you seen such a thing as a Crocodile in these promiscuous parts?"

"*Have* I seen a Crocodile?" said the Bi-Coloured-Python-Rock-Snake, in a voice of dretful scorn. "What will you ask me next?"

" 'Scuse me," said the Elephant's Child, "but could you kindly tell me what he has for dinner?"

Then the Bi-Coloured-Python-Rock-Snake
uncoiled himself very quickly from the
rock and spanked the Elephant's
Child with his scalesome,
flailsome tail.

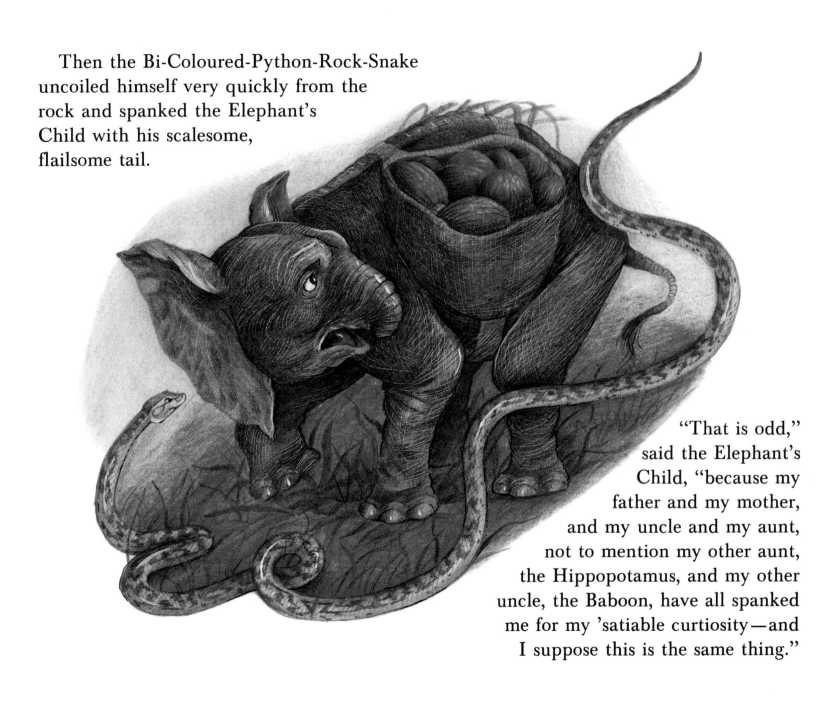

"That is odd,"
said the Elephant's
Child, "because my
father and my mother,
and my uncle and my aunt,
not to mention my other aunt,
the Hippopotamus, and my other
uncle, the Baboon, have all spanked
me for my 'satiable curtiosity—and
I suppose this is the same thing."

So he said good-bye very politely to the Bi-Coloured-Python-Rock-Snake, and helped to coil him up on the rock again, and went on, a little warm, but not at all astonished, eating melons and throwing the rind about, because he could not pick it up, till he trod on what he thought was a log of wood at the very edge of the great grey-green, greasy Limpopo River, all set about with fever-trees.

But it was really the Crocodile,
O Best Beloved, and the Crocodile
winked one eye—like this!

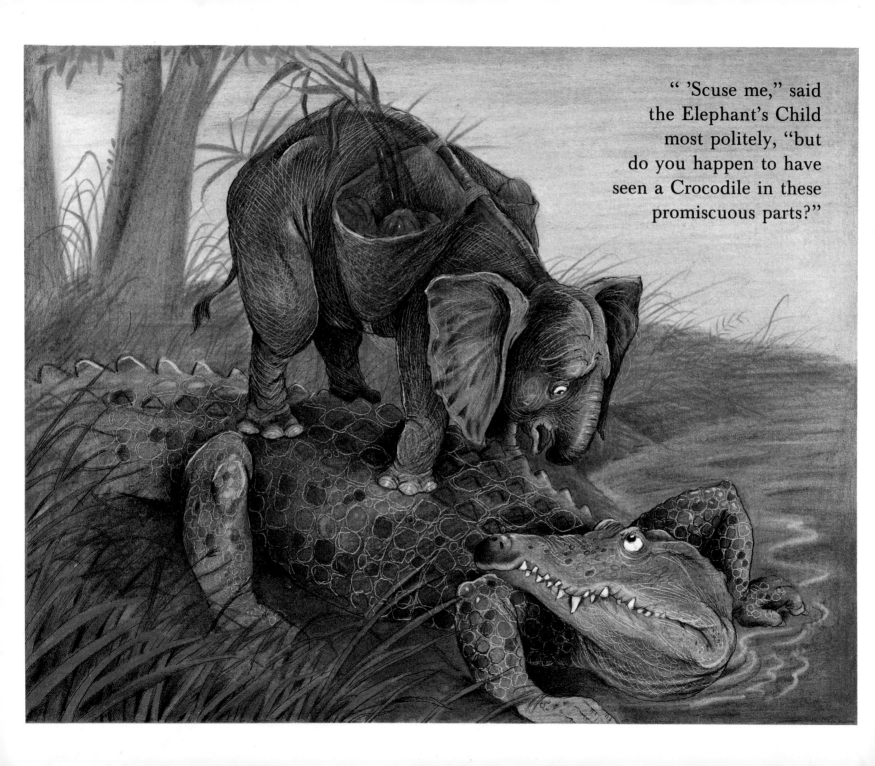

" 'Scuse me," said the Elephant's Child most politely, "but do you happen to have seen a Crocodile in these promiscuous parts?"

Then the Crocodile winked the other eye and lifted half his tail out of the mud; and the Elephant's Child stepped back most politely, because he did not wish to be spanked again.

"Come hither, Little One," said the Crocodile. "Why do you ask such things?"

" 'Scuse me," said the Elephant's Child most politely, "but my father has spanked me, my mother has spanked me, not to mention my tall aunt, the Ostrich, and my tall uncle, the Giraffe, who can kick ever so hard, as well as my broad aunt, the Hippopotamus, and my hairy uncle, the Baboon, *and* including the Bi-Coloured-Python-Rock-Snake, with the scalesome, flailsome tail, just up the bank, who spanks harder than any of them; and *so,* if it's quite all the same to you, I don't want to be spanked any more."

"Come hither, Little One," said the Crocodile, "for I am the Crocodile," and he wept crocodile-tears to show it was quite true.

Then the Elephant's Child grew all breathless, and panted, and kneeled down on the bank and said, "You are the very person I have been looking for all these long days. Will you please tell me what you have for dinner?"

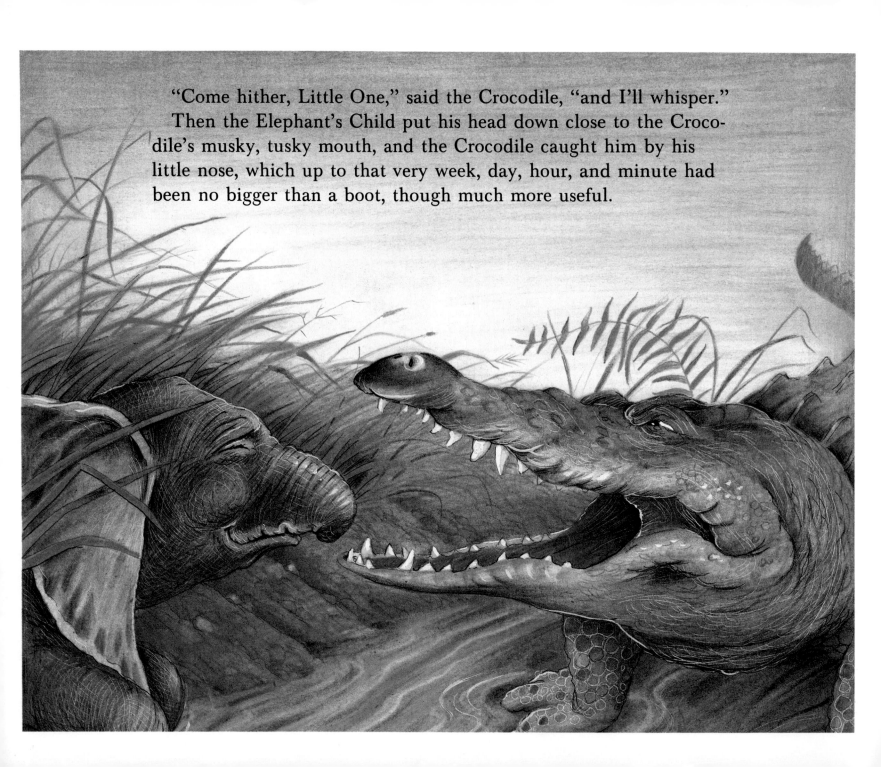

"Come hither, Little One," said the Crocodile, "and I'll whisper." Then the Elephant's Child put his head down close to the Crocodile's musky, tusky mouth, and the Crocodile caught him by his little nose, which up to that very week, day, hour, and minute had been no bigger than a boot, though much more useful.

"I think," said the Crocodile—and he said it between his teeth, like this—"I think today I will begin with Elephant's Child!"

At this, O Best Beloved, the Elephant's Child was much annoyed, and he said, speaking through his nose, like this, "Led go! You are hurtig be!"

Then the Bi-Coloured-Python-Rock-Snake scuffled down from the bank and said, "My young friend, if you do not now, immediately and instantly, pull as hard as ever you can, it is my opinion that your acquaintance in the large-pattern leather ulster" (and by this he meant the Crocodile) "will jerk you into yonder limpid stream before you can say Jack Robinson."

This is the way Bi-Coloured-Python-Rock-Snakes always talk.

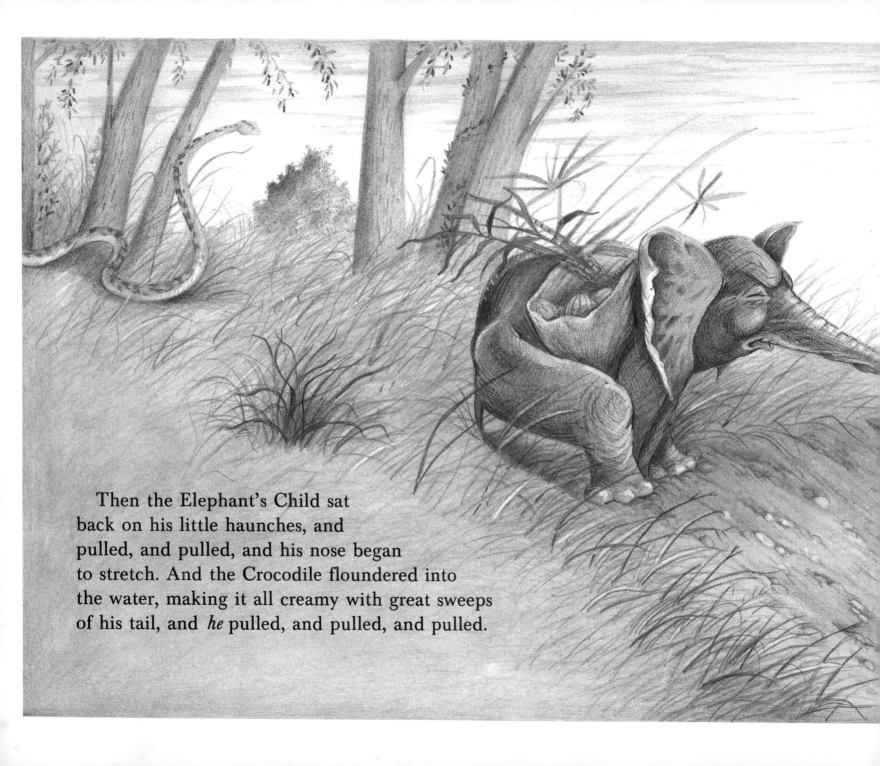

Then the Elephant's Child sat
back on his little haunches, and
pulled, and pulled, and his nose began
to stretch. And the Crocodile floundered into
the water, making it all creamy with great sweeps
of his tail, and *he* pulled, and pulled, and pulled.

And the Elephant's Child's nose kept on stretching; and the Elephant's Child spread all his little four legs and pulled, and pulled, and pulled, and his nose kept on stretching; and the Crocodile threshed his tail like an oar, and *he* pulled, and pulled, and pulled, and at each pull the Elephant's Child's nose grew longer and longer—and it hurt him hijjus!

Then the Elephant's Child felt his legs slipping, and he said through his nose, which was now nearly five feet long, "This is too butch for be!"

Then the Bi-Coloured-Python-Rock-Snake came down from the bank, and knotted himself in a double-clove-hitch round the Elephant's Child's hind legs, and said, "Rash and inexperienced traveller, we will now seriously devote ourselves to a little high tension, because if we do not, it is my impression that yonder self-propelling man-of-war with the armour-plated upper deck" (and by this, O Best Beloved, he meant the Crocodile) "will permanently vitiate your future career."

That is the way all Bi-Coloured-Python-Rock-Snakes always talk.

So he pulled, and the Elephant's Child pulled, and the Crocodile pulled; but the Elephant's Child and the Bi-Coloured-Python-Rock-Snake pulled hardest; and at last the Crocodile let go of the Elephant's Child's nose with a plop that you could hear all up and down the Limpopo.

Then the Elephant's Child sat down most hard
and sudden; but first he was careful to say "Thank
you" to the Bi-Coloured-Python-Rock-Snake; and
next he was kind to his poor pulled nose, and
wrapped it all up in cool banana leaves, and hung
it in the great grey-green, greasy Limpopo to cool.

"What are you doing that for?" said the Bi-Coloured-
Python-Rock-Snake.

" 'Scuse me," said the Elephant's Child, "but
my nose is badly out of shape, and I am waiting
for it to shrink."

"Then you will have to wait a long time," said
the Bi-Coloured-Python-Rock-Snake. "Some
people do not know what is good for them."

The Elephant's Child sat there for three days waiting for his nose to shrink. But it never grew any shorter, and, besides, it made him squint. For, O Best Beloved, you will see and understand that the Crocodile had pulled it out into a really truly trunk same as all Elephants have today.

At the end of the third day a fly came and
stung him on the shoulder, and before he
knew what he was doing, he
lifted up his trunk and
hit that fly dead with
the end of it.

" 'Vantage
number one!"
said the Bi-Coloured-
Python-Rock-Snake. "You
couldn't have done that with a mere-
smear nose. Try and eat a little now."

Before he thought what he was doing,
the Elephant's Child put out his trunk
and plucked a large bundle of
grass, dusted it clean against
his forelegs, and stuffed
it into his own mouth.

" 'Vantage
number two!"
said the Bi-Coloured-
Python-Rock-Snake. "You
couldn't have done that with a mere-
smear nose. Don't you think the sun is very hot here?"

"It is," said the Elephant's Child, and before he thought what he was doing, he schlooped up a schloop of mud from the banks of the great grey-green, greasy Limpopo and slapped it on his head, where it made a cool schloopy-sloshy mud-cap all trickly behind his ears.

" 'Vantage number three!" said the Bi-Coloured-Python-Rock-Snake. "You couldn't have done that with a mere-smear nose. Now how do you feel about being spanked again?"

" 'Scuse me," said the Elephant's Child, "but I should not like it at all."

"How would you like to spank somebody?" said the Bi-Coloured-Python-Rock-Snake.

"I should like it very much indeed," said the Elephant's Child.

"Well," said the Bi-Coloured-Python-Rock-Snake, "you will find that new nose of yours very useful to spank people with."

"Thank you," said the Elephant's Child, "I'll remember that; and now I think I'll go home to all my dear families and try."

So the Elephant's Child
went home across Africa frisking
and whisking his trunk. When he wanted
fruit to eat, he pulled fruit down from
a tree, instead of waiting for it to fall as he used
to do. When he wanted grass, he plucked grass
up from the ground, instead of going on his knees
as he used to do. When the flies bit him, he broke
off the branch of a tree and used it as a fly-whisk;
and he made himself a new, cool, slushy-squshy
mud-cap whenever the sun was hot.

When he felt lonely walking
through Africa, he sang to himself down his trunk, and the noise
was louder than several brass bands. He
went especially out of his way to find a broad
Hippopotamus (she was no relation of his), and
he spanked her very hard, to make sure that the
Bi-Coloured-Python-Rock-Snake had spoken the truth
about his new trunk. The rest of the time he picked
up the melon rinds that he had dropped on his way
to the Limpopo—for he was a Tidy Pachyderm.

One dark evening he came back to all his dear families, and he coiled up his trunk and said, "How do you do?" They were very glad to see him and immediately said, "Come here and be spanked for your 'satiable curtiosity."

"Pooh," said the Elephant's Child. "I don't think you peoples know anything about spanking; but *I* do, and I'll show you."

Then he uncurled his trunk and knocked two of his dear brothers head over heels.

"O Bananas!" said they. "Where did you learn that trick, and what have you done to your nose?"

"I got a new one from the Crocodile on the banks of the great grey-green, greasy Limpopo River," said the Elephant's Child. "I asked him what he had for dinner, and he gave me this to keep."

"It looks very ugly," said his hairy uncle, the Baboon.

"It does," said the Elephant's Child. "But it's very useful," and he picked up his hairy uncle, the Baboon, by one hairy leg and hove him into a hornets' nest.

Then that bad Elephant's Child spanked
all his dear families for a long time, till they
were very warm and greatly astonished. He
pulled out his tall Ostrich aunt's tail-feathers;

and he caught his tall uncle, the Giraffe, by the hind leg and dragged him through a thorn-bush; and he shouted at his broad aunt, the Hippopotamus, and blew bubbles into her ear when she was sleeping in the water after meals; but he never let anyone touch Kolokolo Bird.

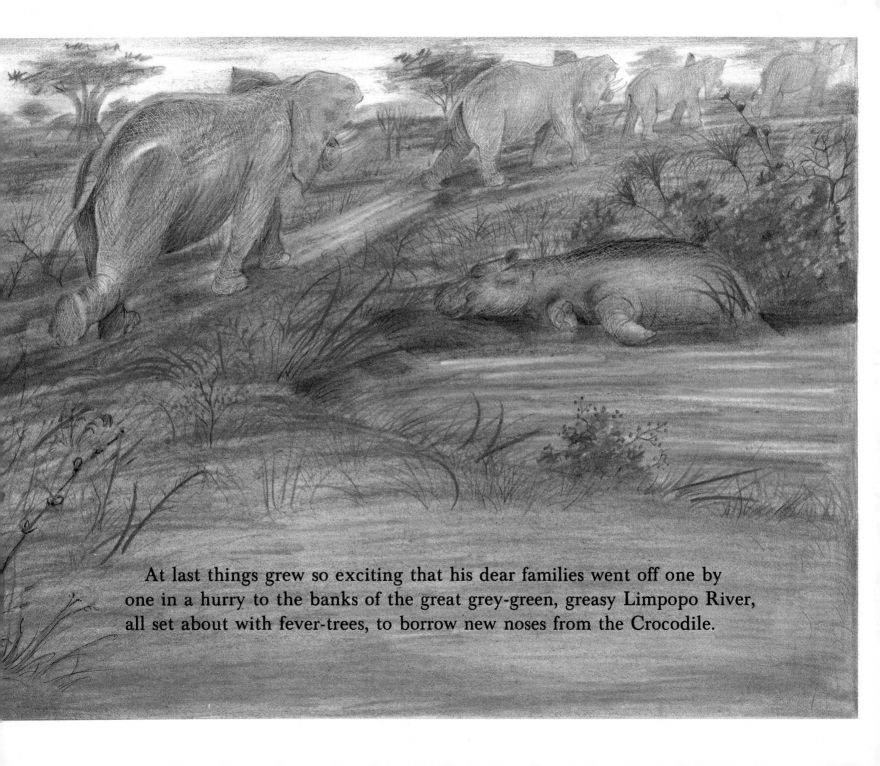

At last things grew so exciting that his dear families went off one by one in a hurry to the banks of the great grey-green, greasy Limpopo River, all set about with fever-trees, to borrow new noses from the Crocodile.

When they came back, nobody spanked anybody any more; and ever since that day, O Best Beloved, all the Elephants you will ever see, besides all those that you won't, have trunks precisely like the trunk of the 'satiable Elephant's Child.